Samuel Stehman Haldeman

Rhymes of the poets

Samuel Stehman Haldeman

Rhymes of the poets

ISBN/EAN: 9783337271220

Printed in Europe, USA, Canada, Australia, Japan

Cover: Foto ©Andreas Hilbeck / pixelio.de

More available books at **www.hansebooks.com**

RHYMES

OF THE

POETS

BY FELIX AGO

But this coxcombically mingling
Of rhymes unrhyming, interjingling,
For numbers genuinely British
Is quite too finical and skittish.   *Byrom.*

PHILADELPHIA:

PUBLISHED BY E. H. BUTLER & CO.

1868

SHERMAN & CO., PRINTERS.

PREFACE

You praise our sires; but though they wrote with force
Their rhymes were vicious, and their diction coarse. *Gifford.*

D R. JOHNSON, in his Plan of an English Dictionary,
says that "Some words have *two sounds* which may be
" equally admitted, as being equally defensible by authority.
" Thus *great* is differently used

" For Swift and him despised the force of state
" The sober follies of the wise and great. *Pope.*

" As if misfortune made the throne her seat,
" And none could be unhappy but the great. *Rowe.*"

It is probable, however, that if one of the two words *seat*
and *great* was perverted, it was *seat*, which has the dialectic
and original pronunciation of *sate*. Gay, who was born in
Devonshire in 1688, probably used this sound, and read the
following examples as true rhymes, without perverting *great*—

Talks of ambition's tott'ring seat, [sate]
How envy persecutes the great,

Excuse me then if pride, conceit,
The manners of the fair and great,

I grant it does; and who's so great,
That has the privilege to cheat? *Gay.*

Doubtless the pleasure is as great
Of being cheāted as to cheāt; *Butler.*

never yŏt
Was dight a masquing half so nĕat, *Parnell.*

I*

In Old English such rhymes are normal, *treat* rhyming
with *great*, and *estate* with *at*, as in—

> And in what wise I will but shortly trete,
> And of this thynge I touchĕ but the grete.　*Chaucer.*

> So valour, in a low estăte,
> Is most admir'd and wonder'd at.　*Butler.*

> 　　　　　　　　　　　hârd, . . .
> And many times surpris'd him unprepâr'd.　*Daniel.*

> Oft with the bêarded spèar
> They . . . slew the angry bêar.　*Drayton.*

> And, like a maggot in a sōre,
> Would that which gave it life devôur;　*Butler.*

> Either I mistake your shape and making quite,
> Or else you are that shrew'd and knavish spirit　*Shak.*

> Now it is the time of night, . . .
> Every one lets forth his spright,　*Shak.*

> To set thy praises in as high a key,
> As France, or Spain, or Germany, or they.　*Drayton.*

> Because I breathe not love to every ōne, . . .
> Nor give each speech a full point of a groan　.*Sidney.*

It is better to spoil a rhyme than a word.　In modern normal English therefore, every word which has a definite sound
and accent in conversation, should retain it in verse; *great*
should never be perverted into *greet* to the ear, *sinned* into
signed, *grinned* into *grind*, or *wind* into *wind*.

A few words have two forms in English speech, as *said*,
which Pope and Th. Moore rhyme with *laid* and *head;* and
again, which Shakespeare, Dryden and Th. Moore rhyme
with *plain* and *then*, and Suckling with *inn*.　*Towards* has

two legitimate forms in poetry, the original terminal accent having been shifted in speech.   Thus Spenser has—

> And ran towàrdes the far rebounded noyce, . . .
> They, seeing Una, tòwardes her gan wend, . . .

The learned Sir William Jones is the purest rhymer known to the author, questionable rhymes being so rare in his verse as not to attract attention.   His ARCADIA of 368 lines has but *forlorn* and *horn; god, rode; wind, behind; mead, reed* (*mead* of *meadow* being *med* and not *meed*.*)   CAISSA of 334 lines, SOLIMA of 104, and LAURA of 150, are perfect.   THE SEVEN FOUNTAINS, of 542 lines, has only *afford* and *lord*.   THE PALACE OF FORTUNE, 506 lines, has only *shone—sun*, and *stood—blood*.   THE ENCHANTED FRUIT, 574 lines, has *wound—ground* twice, which some assimilate.   The few questionable rhymes might have been avoided; and these poems are sufficiently extended to show what can be done in the way of legitimate rhyme.

Versifiers excuse bad rhymes in several ways, as Dr. Garth—

> Ill lines, but like ill paintings, are allow'd
> To set off and to recommend the good:

---

* The daughters of the flood have search'd the mead
For violets pale, and cropp'd the poppy's head, *Dryden.*

Here wanton Mincius winds along the meads,
And shades his happy banks with bending reeds. *Dryden.*

But now we see none here,
Whose silvery feet did tread,
And, with dishevell'd hair,
Adorn'd this smoother mead. *Herrick.*

Brilliant drops bedeck the mead,
Cooling breezes shake the reed; *Johnson.*

but it is doubtful whether the Doctor would thus have asso-
ciated *allow'd* and *good*, if he could have readily procured less
dissonant equivalents. Contrariwise, some authors make effi-
cient use of what to them are allowable rhymes, and much
of the spirit of Hudibras would be lost without them.

> Cardan believ'd great states depend
> Upon the tip o' th' Bear's tail's end ;
> That, as she whisk'd it t'wards the Sun,
> Strew'd mighty empires up and down;
> Which others say must needs be false,
> Because your true bears have no tails. *Butler.*

These pages are made up chiefly from the following (114)
writers.

Addison	Cowper	Habington	Moore, Th.	Smollett
Akenside	Crabbe	Hall, Bp.	Motherwell	Somerville
Barbauld	Crashaw	Hawes	Northcote	South
Barham	Croswell	Hemans	Parnell	Southey
Bayley	Croxall	Herrick	Percival	Spenser
Beattie	Daniel	Hill	Philips	Sydney
Berkeley	Darwin	Hogg	Pierpont	Tennyson
Blackmore	Davenant	Hoole	Pitt	Thackeray
Bowles	Donne	Johnson	Pollok	Thom
Broome	Drayton	Keats	Pope	Thomson
Browne	Drummond	Keble	Praed	Tickell
Bryant	Dryden	Lamb	Prior	Tighe
Bulwer	Dyer	Landon	Proctor	Waller
Burns	Emerson	Longfellow	Robert of	Warner
Butler	Falconer	Lowell	Gloucester	WARRENIANA
Byron	Fawkes	Lyttleton	Rogers	Warton
Campbell	Garth	Mant	Rowe	Watts
Cary	Gay	Marlowe	Savage	White, H. K.
Chaucer	Goldsmith	Mason	Saxe	Whittier
Churchill	Gower	Mathias	Scott	Wiffen
Coleridge	Grant	Milton	Shakespeare	Wordsworth
Cotton	Granville	Montgomery	Shelley	Wyatt
Cowley	Gray	Moore, Edw.	Smith	Young

AIR or EAR.

List, list, I hear
Some far off hallow break the silent aire [ear?]   *Milton*, Comus

With golden pendants in his ears,
Aloft the silken reins he bears, *Fawkes*.

He caught their manners, looks and airs;
An ass in ev'ry thing but ears! *Gay*.

But *beares*—*eares* (hairs—ears) rhyme in

In braded tramels, that no looser heares
Did out of order stray about her daintie eares. *Spenser*.

BARD or BIRD.

As Horoscope urg'd farther to be heard,
He thus was interrupted by a bard [bird.] *Garth*.

Young Selby at the fair hall-board
Carved to his uncle, and that lord,
And reverently took up the word. *W. Scott*.

BLOOD.

Knowing that the South American indjgens (indigens) pronounce English so badly as probably to say *bloo-d* for *blud*;
Bowles (whom Byron terms "an amiable, well-informed,
and extremely able man,") takes advantage of the real or sup-
posable fact as follows—

In sea-wolf's skin, here Mariantu stood;
Gnash'd his white teeth, impatient, and cried "Blood!"

The sublimity which the use of the single word bl-oo-d gives to this passage, produces an effect upon the listener which has scarcely a parallel in English verse, unless it is in Warreniana, but this is aided by the curse which the speaker invokes upon himself—

> ' You chilly blast,' she cried, with heart o'er full,
> But he replied, ' No, blast me if I wooll!'

A New England poet thus "piles on the agony" with a wolfish elongation of the word bloo-oo-d, mollified into *blued*—

> Slavery the earth-born Cyclops fellest of the giant brood,
> Sons of brute force and Darkness who have drenched the earth with
>   blood !

> The dart which in his hand now trembling stood, . . .
> Drew with its daring point celestial blood. *Tighe.*

> And there with glassy gaze she stood
> As ice were in her curdled blood. *Byron.*

> Beneath his ear the fastened arrow stood,
> And from the wound appear'd the trickling blood. *Dryden.*

> With mingled roar resounds the wood;
> Their teeth, their claws distil with blood; *Gay.*

> He pass'd in the heart of that ancient wood,
> The dark shrine stain'd with the victim's blood; *Hemans.*

> The strength of some fierce tenant of the wood . . .
> The beast that prowls abroad in search of blood. *South.*

> Where miscreant hands and rude
> Have stain'd her pure ethereal pall
>   With many a martyr's blood. *Keble*, Prof. of Poetry, Oxford.

Ring out false pride in place and blood . . .
Ring in the common love of good.   *Tennyson.*

There all aghast the shivering wretches stood,
While chill suspense and fear congealed their blood ;   *Falconer.*

Firm in his loyalty he stood
And prompt to seal it with his blood.   *Scott.*

Verbeia then in wild amazement stood
To see her silver urn distained with blood.   *Fawkes.*

Translators are not to be held to the line of propriety with as much strictness as those who are at liberty to choose their words ; but if this prevents us from censuring, it also prevents us from praising certain rhymes, as these of Pope, which might have shared the honors conceded to Bowles.

They throng'd so close, the Grecian squadrons stood
In radiant arms, and thirst for Trojan blood.   Iliad 2 : 559.

Next Teuthras' son distain'd the sands with blood,
Axylus, hospitable, rich, and good.   id. 6 : 15.

Fierce as the mountain lions bathed in blood,
Or foaming boars, the terror of the wood.   id. 7 : 307.

In other cases Pope uses this figure in a manner to remind one of boys who are so anxious to behold the effects of their fire-works, that they set them off unseasonably, namely, during daylight.   Darwin is more judicious—

Vault o'er the plain, and in the tangled wood,
Lo! dead Eliza weltering in her blood!

And so is Byron—

They stood the three, as the three hundred stood
Who dyed Thermopylæ with holy blood.

Even the rats in Hudibras

> Strongly in defence on 't stood
> And from the wounded foe drew blood.

> As slow he winds in museful mood [mud?]
> Near the rush'd marge of Cherwell's flood.   *Warton.*

> His brave contempt of state shall teach the proud
> None but the virtuous are of noble blood : *Garth.*

> High is his couch; the ocean flood . . .
> As round him heaved, while high he stood, *Pierpont.*

> The tresses of the woods, . . .
> And the full-brimming floods, *Percival.*

BREAK or BREEK.

> Of winds and elements on thy head will break,
> And in thy agonising ear the shriek, *H. K. White.*

CARE or CUR.

> Through fate's fantastics mazes errs . . .
> To combat against real cares.   *Prior.*

COME or COMB.

> when he comes home;
> For us your yellow ringlets comb, *Wordsworth.*

The judicious Saxe is represented to have made use of an expression the "true reading" of which may have been misunderstood by the phonographer who took down the address in which it occurs. If, as a New Englander, the speaker said *hum* for *home,* the first version sounds better than the second—which is added under the impression that the vernacular may have been discarded for the more Southern hōme.

> .   .   .   .   .   . golden grains
> Which in the fulness of the year shall cŏme
> In bounteous sheaves, to bless my harvest-hŏme!
> .   .   .   . *golden grains*
> *Which in the fulness of the year shall comb*
> *From bounteous sheaves to bless my harvest bome.*

Compare Barry Cornwall—

> Sound an alarum!   The foe is come!
> I hear the tramp—the neigh—the hum—

Bryant—

> Oh, loveliest there the spring days come,
> With blossoms, and birds, and wild bees' hum—

Herrick—

> With wicker arks did come, . . .
> The richer cowslips home.

Fawkes—

> Should gammar Gurton leave these helps at home,
> To church with Bible, 'tis in vain to come.

Th. Moore—

> In peace, by all who come; . . .
> Some long-lost exile home.

Scott—

> Since to your home
> A destined errant knight I come.

Landon—

> Her temple and her home, . . .
> Whence all her joys must come.

Pope—

> Thence to revisit your imperial dome
> An old hereditary guest I come.

And Dryden—

> Myself will search our planted grounds at hŏme
> For downy peaches and the glossy plum.   Pastoral 2.

> These drudge the fields abroad; and those at home
> Lay deep foundations for the labour'd comb,
> With dew, narcissus-leaves, and clammy gum.   Georg. 4 : 234-6.

As there is no real connexion between a word and its conventional spelling, I have not varied from the ordinary editions, as John Carey, LL.D., has done with Dryden; and various critics and printers with Shakespeare, Milton and others, because the rhyme indicates the pronunciation and this the word.   I may be wrong in giving "bloo-d" when *followed by* "food," where some may prefer "blud," with a corresponding twist in "food;" but the English prosodists consulted are silent on the question of a first line termination forming an "allowable" rhyme to a subsequent one, instead of the reverse.

Bloomfield was addicted to what is with doubtful propriety termed bad spelling, so that his poems, like Shakespeare's, do not appear as he wrote them, except perhaps where his editor mistook a word for a different one.   Hence *comb* may be the proper spelling in the next, where "rosy morn" is equivalent to Aurora—

> This task had Giles in fields remote from home
> Oft has he wished the rosy morn to come—

thus imitated by W. M. Thackeray—

> To a fair mistress and a pleasant home
> Where soft hearts greet us whensoe'er we come.
> (*Where soft beads greet us whensoe'er we comb.*)

And by the Yankee philosopher, in the Yankee dialect—

> To those who go and those who come
> Good-by, proud world, I'm going home [hum !]

DEEP or DIP.

> So with resistless haste the wounded ship [sheep ?]
> Scuds from pursuing waves along the deep : [dip ?]   *Falconer.*

DENYING or DEN-YING.

In the next quatrain, illiterate readers would suppose that the adjoined—the alternate—or the whole of the lines, were intended to rhyme, but so far from this being the fact, the specimen belongs to a poem in which the fourth line rhymes with the first, and the third with the second, proving that poets are quite too deep for common people.   It will be observed that den-*ying* is used as a dissyllable, and d-*ying* as a monosyllable, like *jing'* for *jingle.*

> Of transient joys that ask no STING
> From jealous fears, or coy den*ying*
> But born beneath love's brooding *wing*,
> And into tenderness soon dYING.   *Coleridge.*

" Love's brooding wing " turns the little fellow into an old hen.

> Some légates sent from the Molossian state
> Were on a peaceful errand come to treat,
> Of these he murders one, he boils the flesh
> And lays the mangled morsels in a dish,

Some part he roasts, then serves it up so dress'd
And bids me welcome to this human feast.   *Dryden.*

Surely all Æol's huffing brood
Are met to war against the flood,
Which seem surpris'd, and have not yet
Had time his levies to complete.   *Cotton.*

Action and life from ev'ry part are gone
And e'en her entrails turn to solid stone ;
Yet still she weeps, and whirl'd by stormy winds,
Borne through the air her native country finds,
Where high on Sipylus's shaggy brow
She stands her own sad monument of woe.   *Croxall.*

The authors of these monstrosities *allow* them to stand under the appellation of "allowable" rhymes, and ordinary writers and speakers are so good-natured as to permit their language to be thus gibbeted and pilloried, although the pronunciatorial executioners of English words are unacquainted with the philosophic principles which govern variations of language.

FEAR or FARE.

The lookers-on, (for lookers-on there were,)
Shock'd at the sight, half died away with fear.   *Eusden.*

FLED or FLAY'D.

But that her ancient spirit is decay'd,
That sacred wisdom from her bounds is fled.   *Lyttleton.*

GRASS or GRACE.

So we mistake the future's fâce
Eyed through Hope's deluding glâss.   *Campbell.*

Our sports Acestes of the Trojan rûce   [Arab. rûs *bead.*]
With royal gifts ordain'd, is pleased to grâce   *Dryden.*

HEVN or HIVN.

Some sense, and more estate, kind heaven
To this well lotted peer has given. *Prior.*

HILLS or HEELS.

The pensive poet thro' the green-wood steals, [stills?] . . .
Or climbs the steep ascent of airy hills; [heels?] *Warton.*

HOARD or HERD.

New milk, and clouted cream, mild cheese and curd,
With some remaining fruit of last year's hoard, *Phillips.*

JOIN or JINE.

But wit's like a luxuriant vine:
Unless to virtue's prop it join, *Cowley.*

So mulishly absurd as not to join
In this with me, save always thee and thine. *Gifford.*

See with the fire of youth how art combines
When Milton's muse with Westall's pencil joins. *Mathias.*

This said they all engaged to join
Their forces in the same design. HUDIBRAS.

Or where, all dreadful in th' embattled line,
The hostile ships in flaming combat join. *Falconer.*

Good nature and good sense must ever join;
To err is human; to forgive, divine. *Pope.*

2*

In praise so just let every voice [vice ?] be joined
And fill the general chorus of mankind. *Pope.*

From cliff to cliff the foaming torrents shine
While waters, woods, and winds in concert join. *Beattie.*

The heart whose impulse stay'd not for the mind
To freeze to doubt what charity enjoined. *Bulwer.*

So lines that from their parallel decline,
More they proceed the more they still disjoin. *Garth.*

So when the sun to west was far declin'd
And both afresh in mortal combat join'd. *Dryden.*

Each tender pledge of sacred faith he join'd,
Each gentler pleasure of th' unspotted mind. *Coleridge.*

In after-times as courts refin'd
Our patriots in the list were join'd. *Tickell.*

Me too his power has reached, and bids with thine
My rustic pipe in pleasing concert join. *Lyttleton.*

———

The passive gods beheld the Greeks defile
Their temples, and abandon to the spoil. *Dryden.*

Heedless of this, but with a pitying sigh . .
He shed in haste the balmy drops of joy *Tighe.*

        orient skies !
Riches denied, thy boon was purer joys, *Burns.*

To me in vain, on earth's prolific soil,
With summer crown'd the Elysian valleys smile. *Falconer.*

Of hot ambition, irreligion's ice,
Zeal's agues, and hydropic avarice, *Donne.*

As in some old cathedral's glimmering aisle [oil ?]
The dusty monuments from light recoil.* *Byron.*

LOIN or LINE.

Conjunction, preposition, adverb join
To stamp new vigour on the nervous line : *Churchill.*

LOOV, LOAVE or LUV.

Rare artisan, whose pencil moves
Not our delights alone, but loves ! *Waller.*

On Leven's banks, while free to rove,
And tune the rural pipe to love ; *Smollett.*

               love, . . .
Far in the nameless mountain cove. *Keble.*

          where'er they move,
From hopes fulfill'd and mutual love. *Keble.*

Through tracts aloft on daring pinions rove,
Where'er by duty borne, or led by love . . . .
Yet all shall read and all the page approve
When public spirit meets with public love. Purs. of Lit.

Dumb swans, not chattering pies, do lovers prove :
They love indeed, who quake to say they love. *Sir Ph. Sydney.*

For a gate of five bars will certainly prove
An effectual bar to my being in love. *T. H. Bayley.*

But, as from string to string I move,
My lute will only sound to love. *Philips.*

---

* Their *resile* must be owing to their resilience.

The bird, as if my questions did her move,
With trembling wings sigh'd forth, I love, I love   *Drummond.*

Oh, then, how sweet to move . . .
Led by light from eyes we love.   *Tb. Moore.*

If these delights thy mind may move,
Then live with me, and be my love.   *Marlowe.*

The reeds scarce rustle, nor the aspens move,
And all the feathered folks forbear their lays of love.   *Garth.*

Unborn to cherish, sneakingly approves :
And wants the soul to spread the worth he loves.   *Hill.*

her bondage prove
The fetters of a dream, opposed to love.   *Wordsworth.*

Oh, mornin' life! oh, mornin' luve.   *Motherwell.*

Then hastens onward to the pensive grove,
The silent mansion of disastrous love.   *Garth.*

Near the chequer'd, lonely grove,
Hears, and keeps thy secrets, love !   *Johnson.*

When, sleeping in the grove,
He dreamed not of her love.   *Longfellow.*

But fairer is the smile of one we love, . . .
And sweeter than the music of the grove, *Southey.*

Then just the hot and stony beach above,
Light twinkling streams in bright confusion move.   *Crabbe.*

Or crawls beside the coral grove,
And hears the ocean roll above; *Gay.*

The lime-leaf waves not in the grove, . . .
The birds have ceased their songs of love, *Hemans.*

Morn or Mourn.

I have worn, . . .
Joyed at the opening splendour of the morn,   *Southey.*

One or Won.

There was one
Whom she lov'd in days now gone.   *Landon.*

If song be past, and hope undone
It is thy work, thou faithless one.   *Landon.*

Pant or Paint.

When in the sultry glebe I faint,
Or on the thirsty mountain pant,   *Addison.*

Rome, Room or Rum.

For Eleuthere a god man was the Pope of Rome,
Thorw wam first christene men into Englond com.
                              Robert of Gloucester.

What can our travellers bring home,
That is not to be learnt at Rome?   *Butler.*

That durst upon a truth give doom,
He knew less than the Pope of Rome.   *Butler.*

And from a scavenger did come
To be a mighty prince of Rome.   *Butler.*

Thus when we view some well-proportioned dome,
The world's just wonder, and e'en thine oh Rome.   *Pope.*

From the same foes, at last, both felt their doom,
And the same age saw learning fall, and Rome.   *Pope.*

Time has but touched, not sealed in gloom
The turrets of almighty Rome. *Wiffen.*

But not to Greece—but not to Rome
  These spells alone belong,
Each sod, each wave was glory's home
   Where honour spurned at wrong. *Wiffen.*

Thus murmuring to himself: wilt thou to Rome
Base as thou art, and seek thy lazy home? *Rowe.*

Sighs o'er each broken urn and yawning tomb,
And mourns the fall of Liberty and Rome. *Darwin.*

These thoughts are for the state, enough of Rome
Her gallic altars, and approaching doom, [dome!] . . .

Yea, sweet it is to them, afar to roam . . .
And to the mother land of Christendom *Bp. Mant.*

But if from themes so grave you never roam,
Ask at St. Paul's is Prettyman at home, *Mathias,* Purs. of Lit.

What gorgeous trophies crown his youthful bloom,
The spoils august of Athens and of Rome! *Grant.*

There the dread phalanx of Reformers come,
Sworn foes to wit, as Carthage was to Rome: [rum!] *Garth.*

And threatened them all with the judgment to cŏme
Of a wandering star's first impressions of Rŏme. *Lowell.*

As Hannibal did to the altars come,
Swore by his sire a mortal foe to Rŏme;

  .   .   .   .   come
Like Goths and Vandals to demolish Rŏme. *Dryden.*

Room or Rum, or Roam.

Troops of right-honourable porters come,
And garter'd small-coal merchants crowd the room. *Pitt.*

Besides as exiles ever from your homes, . . .
Contending, thrusting, shuffling for your rooms*
Of ease or honour, *Daniel*, b. 1562.

Descend their dusky roomes ;* . . .
Adiorn'd to after-domes. *Warner.*

Shares or Shears.

A conventicle flesh'd his greener years,
And his full age the righteous rancour shares [shears?] *Garth.*

'Tis with concern, my friends! I meet you here;
No grievance you can know but I must share [sheer?] *Garth.*

A sigil in his hand the gipsy bears,
In th' other a prophetic sieve and sheers. *Garth.*

Shine or Shin.

The following stanza, taken from a little American Sunday-school book, is descriptive of the sun, and displays the genius of the poet. Knowing that we may take suitable words from foreign languages, he virtually prefers the French *est* to the English *east*. Hudibras could prove

A calf an alderman, a goose a justice
And rooks committee-men and trustees—

and as the revising committee might object to the profane

---

* True rhymes.

word *to shin*, the poet hides it under the externals of *shine*,
shrewdly guessing that the occasional stolidity of committee-
men would prevent them from perceiving that the allusion to
a *race*, and the collateral facts that the runner ' never *tires*
nor *stops* to *rest*,' clearly represent the Old Sôl as shinning it
round the world.

> When from the chambers of the E^aST
> His morning race beGINS,
> He never tires nor stops to REST
> But round the world he SHIN^eS.

In old English *rest* and *est* formed a true rhyme—

> And at the laste, when Phebus in the west . . .
> When cleare Dyana in the fayre southest   *Hawes*, 15 Cent.

> Abate thy houres, shine comfort from the East, . . .
> From these that my poore companie detest; *Shak.*

> So age a mature mellowness doth set
> On the green promises of youthful heat. *Denham*, b. 1615.

According to another Sunday-school specimen—

> It is a sin
> To steal a pin,
> Much more to steal
> A greater thing—

(as a nutmeg grater), the rhyme of which did not satisfy the
uncorrupted ear of the pupils, who accordingly improved it
somewhat thus—

> It is a sin   It is a sin
> To steal a pin,   To steal a pin,
> A nutmeg grate 'r   It is a greater
> Sweet potater—   To steal a 'tater—

It is a venial sin
To steal a menial pin
or,   It is a sin more mortal
To steal a snappin' tortle—

'tater being poetic for potato.   The emendations are worthy
of being placed beside

"The mighty king Senacherib
"On every man could crack a rib
"Excepting king Jehosaphat
"He could not his he was so fat."

SWORD or SWARD.

warlike lords
Lay mail'd in armour, girt in ireful swords.   *Drayton*.

TOIL or TILE.

We cannot tell whether the tile referred in the next is the
square-topt university cap, thus named (see Hogarth's print of
the Lecture,) or that part of the roof which the rays of the
sun first strike—

On all thy hours security shall smile
And bless thine evening walk and morning toil.   *Dr. Johnson*.

Use every art of words and winning smiles
To allure the leader Godfrey to thy toils: *Hoole*.

And ancient faith that knows no guile,
And industry imbrown'd with toil.   *Smollett*.

O'er whose blue bosom rose the starry isles;
The healthy slumber, earn'd by sportive toils.   *Byron*.

Meaning such tiles as are used in pitching quoits?
3

TONE, TOON or TOWN.

If an English lexicographer does not know what a *town* is called, instead of asking his washerwoman or his bootblack, he consults some poet who is interested in deceiving him ; and if two poets do not agree, he imagines that the one who writes the best poetry must pronounce the best, and would therefore be likely to prefer Dryden to Gay—

> The female senate was assembled soon
> With all the mob of women of the town. *Dryden.*

> You who the sweets of rural life have known
> Despise th' ungrateful hurry of the town [ton ?] *Gay.*

> For me ? I've less romance, I own,
> Since first my pity shock'd the town ; *L. T. Berguer,*
> Trifles in Verse, Edinb. 1817.

> The spreading branches made a goodly show,
> And full of opening blooms was every bough. *Dryden.*

> 'Tis storm ; and, hid in mist from hour to hour,
> All day the floods a deepening murmur pour ; *Wordsworth.*

> On the luxurious lap of Flora thrown
> On beds of yielding vegetable down.   Purs. of Lit.

> With songs the jovial hinds return from plow ;
> And unyok'd heifers, loitering homeward, low. *Philips.*

> Since to your uncompounded atoms you
> Figures in number infinite allow, *Blackmore.*

> His auburn locks on either shoulder flow'd
> Which to the funeral of his friend he vow'd. *Dryden.*

Tongues or Tongs.

Our loftiest thoughts and loudest songs ; . . .
Hosanna from ten thousand tongues. *Watts.*

Tossed or Toast.

Till, in a fated hour, on Thraci.'s coast
She saw her lover's lifeless body tossed [toast ?] *Falconer.*

On a stern and rock-bound coast ;
Their giant branches tossed ; *Hemans.*

War or ***.

Then marked they, dashing broad and far,
The broken billows of the war, *Scott.*

Like a glory from afar,
First shall head the flock of war ! *Wordsworth.*

Our isle enjoys, by your successful care,
The pomp of peace amidst the woes of war. *Garth.*

The foes are friends, in social league they dare
On Britain to "let slip the dogs of war." *Mason.*

I grant, that, men continuing what they are,
Fierce, avaricious, proud, there must be war. *Cowper.*

Hoarse barks the wolf, the vulture screams from far
The angel Pity shuns the walks of war. *Darwin.*

Wheel a wide circle, form in hollow square,
And now they front, and now they fly the war. *Darwin.*

Of all the trophies gather'd from the war
What shall return ? The conqueror's broken car ! [cor !] *Byron.*

From which a bloody pennant stretched afar
Its comet tail denouncing ample war. *Falconer.*

There the Norman sails afar
Catch the winds and join the war.   *Gray.*

He felt the influence of malignant star
And waged with Fortune an eternal war.   *Beattie.*

A fairer than Venus prepares
To encounter a greater than Mars.   *Granville.*

Ah! what avails it, that, from slavery far [fair?]
I draw the breath of life in English air;   *Johnson.*

For Jove the heart alone regards;
He punishes what man rewards.   *Gay.*

Calm is my soul nor apt to rise in arms
Except when fast approaching danger warns.   *Goldsmith.*

WEIGHT or WIGHT.

My feet, through wine unfaithful to their weight,
Betray'd me tumbling from a towery height,   *Pope.*

Deep rolling from the watery volume's height
The tortur'd sides seem bursting from their weight.   *Falconer.*

The turning of *weight* into *wight*, and *receipt* into *recite*, would justify the perversion of *neither* into *nighther*, as used by half-educated Hibernian waiters, in contradistinction to the illiterate, whose *nayther* is less objectionable. Those who are imperfectly acquainted with English, fancy that the *language* should be controlled by the conventionalities of *spelling;* whereas, one word cannot be pronounced according to the spelling of another word; nor can the French spelling of *colonel* and *lieutenant* exclude the r and f from the English words, as some unmilitary Americans suppose.

WIND or TWIST.

Whiles his false broker lieth in the wind,
And for a present chapman is assigned, *Bp. Hall.*

You limeless sands, loose driving with the wind,
In future cauldrons useful texture find, *Savage.*

With devious steps, now in, now out, doth wind,
Flies what he seeks, and meets what he declin'd,
Lost in the errour of ambiguous ways. *Sherburn.*

WOOD or WUD.

Far beyond the Atlantic floods, . . .
Realms of mountains, dark with woods, *J. Montgomery.*

While stray'd my eyes o'er Towy's flood
Over mëad and over wood, *Dyer.*

Where faire Feronia honour'd in the woods,
And all the deities that haunt the floods, *Browne.*

Why was not I a liver in the woods,
Or citizen of Thetis' crystal floods. *Drummond.*

One rock amid the weltering floods, . . .
One changeless pine in fading woods; *Keble.*

WORD or WARD.

I only wake the softest chord [curd?]
One low, one love-touched whispering word, [ward?] *Landon.*

3*

DIALECTS.

In imitation of the Greeks, some of the poets vary their verses by the use of dialectic forms, as Scotch—

> As still was her look, and as still was her ee,
> As the stillness that lay on the emerant sea.   *James Hogg.*

> The good light of morning is sweet to the E'E
> But ghost gathering midnight, thou'rt dearer to me.   *Wm. Thom.*

> Set are his teeth, his fading EyE
> Is sternly fixed on vacancy.   *Scott.*

> Hath stopped, and fixed its large full EyE
> Upon the lady Emily; [Emma Lee? Lye?]   *Wordsworth.*

> Furious he drove and upward cast his EyE,
> Where next the queen was placed his Emily.   *Byron.*

> (And after rode the quene and Emilie.   *Chaucer.*)

> Upon his hurt she looks so stedfastly, . . .
> And then she reprehends her mangling EyE,   *Shakesp.*

> And smallĕ foulĕs maken melodie
> That slepen allŏ night with open eye.   *Chaucer.*

> Picturing all the rustic's joy
> When boundless plenty greets his eye,   *Kirke White.*

> Oft had he stolen a glance to spy
> How Roderic brook'd his minstrelsY.   *Scott.*

> Poetic visions charm my closing eye . . . .
> Shift to wild notes of sweetest minstrelsY.   *Rogers.*

> key
> To golden palaces, strange minstrelsY,   *Keats.*

In these English forms it is difficult for the audience to determine whether *minstrel's eye* or *minstrel sigh* is meant; but as the English grammar example of false syntax—"Disappointment *sink* the heart of man, but the renewal of hope brings consolation"—is turned into good grammar when written—"Disappointment*s* *ink* the heart of man," i. e., render it black and gloomy, the critical reader will perceive *minstrel's eye* to be as correct as *jealous eye* in—

> As stung his heart, and made his marrow fry
> With burning rage, and frantic jealousy. *Pope.*

The crystal tear drop fills mine e'e [my knee?] *Charles Doyne Sillery, Esq.,*

who may have seen the synovia which lubricates the knee of a calf. In the next, the Scotch word *coom* is used with more knowledge than effect—

> The basset table spread, the tallier come;
> Why stays Smilinda in the dressing room? *Pope.*

> I marked with secret joy the opening bloom
> Of virtue prescient of the fruits to come. *Gifford.*

> And these words shall then become
> Like oppressions thundered doom. *Shelley.*
> (Thundered dumb? or thunderdom?)

Gay prefers the Irish dialect (Old English)—

> Should you the wide encircling net display
> And in its spacious arch enclose the sea . . .
> It would extend the growing theme too long,
> And tire the reader with the watery song. Rural Sports.

> And sentenc'd to retain my nature,
> Transform'd me to this crawling creature; Fable II.

He lost his friends, his practice fail'd;
Truth should not be always reveal'd; Fable XVIII.

My name is Vanity, I sway
The utmost islands of the sea; *Moore*, Fables.

Whose rapid wings thy flight convey,
Through air, and over earth and sea; *Warton*.

A moment snatched the shining form away,
And all was covered with the curling sea. *Pope*.

Behind him far upon the purple waves [weaves?]
The waters waft it, and the nymph receives. [re-saves?]   *Pope*.

The salmons, and some more as well as they,
Now love the Freshets, and then love the sea. *Browne*.

The stoutest vessel to the storm gave way,
And suck'd through loosen'd planks the rushing sea.   *Dryden*.

I am monarch of all I survey, . . .
From the centre, all round to the sea; *Cowper*.

Since by no acts I therefore can defeat
The happy enterprises of the great,   *Garth*.

                    Unthinking fowl!
While those blind flatterers swell thy soul   *Northcote*.

Nor the soliloquy of the hermit owl,
Exhaling all the solitary soul. *Byron*.

A feeling that upbraids the heart
With happiness beyond desert. *Coleridge*.

The rising morning can't assure . . .
For death stands ready at the door, *Watts*.

Or onward where the rude Carinthian boor
Against the houseless stranger shuts the door.   *Goldsmith*.

He comes to Lane, finds garret shut,
Then, not with knuckle, but with foot
He rudely thrusts. *Davenant.*

Yet you have no pretence to strut
With such a voice and such a foot. *Northcote.*

This night his treasured heaps he means to steal,
And what a fund of charity would fail. *Parnell.*

———

Parnell likes a French rhyme—

The graces stand in sight, a satire train,
Peeps o'er their heads, and laughs behind the scene—

So does Dryden—

Nor silence is within, nor voice express,
But a deaf noise of sounds that never cease.

And Pope—

Some thought it mounted to the lunar sphêre,
Since all things lost on earth are treasur'd thêre.

And Addison—

And sometimes casts his eye upon the EᵃST
And sometimes looks on the forbidden wEST.

Habington uses English, French, and German in one trip-
let—

No north wind shall inFEST
But the soft spirit of the EᵃST
Our scent with perfumed banquet FEᵃST.

Mainwaring judiciously uses the Welsh word *cam* (crooked) in connection with *ram's horns*, and also the Persian word for a *cow*—

> Jove (so she sung) was changed into a RAM,
> From whence the horns of Lybian Ammon CAM^e;
> Bacchus a goat; Apollo was a CRO^w;
> Phœbe a cat; the wife of Jove a CO^w,
> Whose hue was whiter than the falling SNO^w.

In the next, the German and old English words Feld and Fest (both used by Chaucer*) are introduced in English orthography for the benefit of the unlearned—

> Who now laments but Palamon compelled
> No more to try the fortune of the F^iELD. *Dryden.*

>   , it rolls around the F^iELD;
> So rolled the float, and so its texture held : [healed?] *Pope.*

> Picus who once th' Ausonian sceptre held,
> Could rein the steed, and fit him for the field. *Garth.*

>   And now the victims drest,
> They draw, divide, and celebrate the FE^aST. *Pope.*

> For her the artist shuns the fuming FE^aST,
> The midnight roar, the Bacchanalian guest, *Mason.*

> Honors the princely chiefs, rewards the rest,
> And holds for thrice three days a royal FE^aST. *Dryden.*

This is properly succeeded by a fast—

---

* The battaille in the feld betwixt hem twaine ...
Why schuld I sowen draf out of my FEST
When I may sowe whete, if that me LEST ? *Chaucer.*

He came, where he this hoste behelde,
And that was in a largĕ felde. *Gower.*

.　.　.　Enjoyment past,
The savage hunger'd for a F●AST; *Edw. Moore.*

We find French used in Shakespeare's epitaph, in which the pronunciation and spelling (plâst) of the day are correct—

STAY PASSENGER, WHY GOEST THOV SO FAST
READ IF THOV CANST WHOM ENVIOVS DEATH HATH PLAST

Ben Jonson uses a similar rhyme correctly—

Before this work? where envy hath not cast
A trench against it, nor a battry plac'd.

The royal judge, on his tribunal plac'd
Who had beheld the fight from first to last. *Dryden.*

Nor is Hebrew neglected—

Attend, unconquer'd maid! accord my vows,
Bid the great hear, and pitying bear my woes. *Pope.*

The face of things is changed, and Athens now
That *laugh'd* so late, becomes the scene of *woe. Byron.*

If *wow* is used for *howl*, as an antithesis to *laugh*, the curious reader will consult the affinities of the Greek, βαὔζω (bowzdo), not forgetting the scholium in Warreniana—

She bark'th her chorus of bow wow WOW
Bow for the quarters and *wow* for the HOUr—
(Four for the quarters and twelve for the hour.—*Coleridge.*)

nor overlook the fact that the effect of bow wow wow is due to a (Canis) molossus. Wenzel (Ueber die Sprache der Thiere) gives some examples which show that German dogs do not bark English—

" Pafpafknurpafpaf, knur, knur, paf, pif."

So the frogs in Rollenhagen's Froschmäseler (1672) speak
a somewhat different language from those of Aristophanes
and Homer—

> Rieffen das hat gethan gar gecksch—
> Koachs, Wrecke, Vky, Kekechs:
> Ryller, Tryller, Kulo, Tulunck !
> Das beklaget sich alt und junck.

English being tolerably adapted to the use of the profane,
we need not wonder that to the frogs of Vesperia should be
attributed a dialect like

> Zoûnds ! blûd-n-cûns ! Rûm ! Môre rûm !
> Pŏte ! knŭe dŏep ! Pŏte ! knŭe dŏep !

It will be observed that the big ones use the base molossus,
and the little ones the treble tribrach.

Barham, a genial and witty writer, but who, unfortunately,
must have learnt his Greek in England, says in his Ingoldsby
Legends

> That an ancient Welsh poet one PYNDAR AP TUDOR
> Was right in proclaiming "ARISTON MEN U-DOR!"

which shows that he never learnt to spell "the languages,"
and pronounce the Welsh *y* and *u*. His Udor should have
been (a Greek) *hydor*, with which (a French) Tudôr would
rhyme. But his pronunciation is as bad as his spelling, turning νοῦς (mind) into ναῦς, a ship.

> His Pa's wedded spouse
> She questions his νους. *Barham.*

> Thine is the genuine head of many a house [hoos? hô-ws?]
> And much divinity without a Νους ! *Pope.*

> Our bard pursued his old A. B. C.
> In fullest sense his name 'Εστησε. *Coleridge.*

" His name," i. e., its initials S. T. C !, if Greek may be thus perverted.

Until they say [thay] " He calleth thee"
        " Θάρσει ἐγείραι φωνεῖ σε !"—*Longfellow.*

Tell be, by Buse, cad *this*  be Greek ?

The authors of such attempts at jingle deserve a νοῦς of a different kind, somewhat like that with which infected districts are enclosed, and known by the name of

CORDON SANITAIRE.

These are as bad as rhyming *noose* or no-ws (with short *o* in *note*) and *house*, instead of house and ναῦς. Swift understood the pronunciation of Chinese—

But let me now awhile survey
Our madam o'er her evening *tea—*

also Pope

Here thou great Anna whom three realms obey,
Dost sometimes counsel take, and sometimes *tea—*

better than Barham

I hardly need say
The Hong merchants had not yet invented How Qua—

4

who is equally unfortunate with Latin —

> But still on these words of the Bard kept his fix'd eye
> INGRATUM SI DIXERIS, OMNIA DIXTI*——

but he does understand the accent of Wyandot, contrary to the practice of certain literary snobs who fancy that there is such a word as Níagára. The Wyandot word, in Latin or German orthography, (with the Hebrew or Arabic hamza,) is Gjă'ᵣ̆ără, the *r* smooth, the three vowels short (as in *cart*,) with the first accented. In the English adaptation, the illiterate read the first syllable *nigh* instead of *knee*.

> And the rain came down in such sheets as would stagger a
> Bird for a simile short of Niágara. *Barham*

which is imitative of Thom. Moore's

> Were taking instead of rope pistol or dagger a
> Desperate dash down the falls of Niagara—

The Knickerbocker Magazine (April, 1855, p. 332,) perverts the pronunciation of Lădŏgă, the first syllable of which is accented by the Russians, and of Ukrain—

> From gray Ladoga to green Ukraine
> And other parts of the Russian domain!

Byron seems to prefer *Spine* to *Spain*—

> How kindly would he send the mild Ukraine,
> With all her pleasant pulks to lecture Spain [spine?] Age of Bronze.

---

* That the Britons did not speak this jargon formerly is evident from a passage in Hermolaeus, written in 1492, and printed in 1534—

ABUNDAT INSULA BRITANIA HOC GENERE : IN HODIERNUMQUE DIEM
BARBARI ILLI UOCE ROMANA UTUNTUR

Churchill is equally severe on French—

> Next came the treasurer of either house
> One with full purse, t'other with not a *sous*.

C. A. P., author of an excellent " Pastoral Ballad after the manner of Shenstone" (in the New York Spirit of the Times,) seems not to know that the orthography of Shang-hæ is Portuguese, and that it consequently rhymes with *high*, like the Latin diphthong *Æ*, so that

> Ye shepherds so cheerful and gay
>
> . . . .
>
> Say, have you observed a Shanghai ?

might have been rendered

> You shepherds so cheerful and spry
> Say, have you observed a Shanghæ?

Professor Longfellow has laid himself out in Chippeway, with a hero whose name, Hiawatha, a Chippeway cannot pronounce, and a versification *not adapted to the language.*

> Heard
> With ⎱
> Sat ⎰ the squirrel adjidaumo
> Spring

where *mo* (nasalised like French *mon*) is the accented syllable, whilst *dau* (*au* for Italian ŭ) is unaccented. The nasal *o* occurs in the two following, where the final (French ê) is distinctly accented.

> And he said to the kenozha [long-snouted]
> To the pike the maskinozha [big long-snouted]

Not having seen a Chippeway since the publication of Hiawatha, whether the effect of these perversions has been to

produce rage or laughter, cannot be stated here.   But it may
be presumed similar to the effect upon a Roman ear which a
modern *Professor* of " Latin" would produce in reading

ARMA VIRUMQUE CANO′ (instead of CA′NO)

in spite of Prisc^kian's assertion that no Latin word has the
accent final.

———

If mineralogists and geologists are allowed to talk of the
crust of the earth, and to have their stilbite, apatite, table-
spar, mineral-tallow, pudding-stone, asparagus-stone, milk-
quartz, ōōlite, berg-mehl, resinite, and pisolite, why should
not as great a poet as Pope be allowed to call a crag or decliv-
ity a *press o' pies ?*

> Which out of nature's common order rise
> The shapeless rock, or hanging precipice.

Byron prefers a *can o' pie*—

> Wide it was and high,
> And show'd a self-born Gothic canopy.

Thackeray is too keen an observer to write a *flat awry*—

> Stranger! I never wrote a flattery,
> Nor signed a page that registered a lie.

Somerville had a *pill awry*—

> No perjur'd villain nail'd on high
> And pelted in the pillory,

and Praed would hold a rose *awry*—

> He gazed on the river that gurgled by . . .
> He clasped his gilded *rosary*.

Odours, when sweet violets die,
Live within the memory. *Shelley*.

Scott's hero stained the floor with *brandy*—

Full in the midst, his Cross of Red
Triumphant Michael brandished . . .
And threw on the pavement a bloody stain.

Croswell allows a choice between *festive all*, and *festive
hall*—

And from the temple wall
Wave verdure o'er the joyful throngs
That crowd his festival.

Emerson's faith was *early a rope*—(see p. 37.)

The sun set, but set not his hope:
Stars rose; his faith was earlier up;

Byron's angels prefer pacing to flying—

Poland! o'er which the avenging angel pass'd
But left thee as he found thee, still a waste.

Softens Deucalion's flinty race,
And tunes the warring world to peace. *Edw. Moore*, Fab. XVI.

And now two nights and now two days were pāst [paste]
Since wide he wander'd on the watery waste. *Pope*.

RHYME.

The next specimens of words "allowed" to rhyme are of
such a nature as to form blank verse, if read as they ought to
be, with the vulgar pronunciation.

Matthew met Richard, when or where
From story is not mighty clear;

4*

Of many knotty points they spoke,
And *pro* and *con* by turns they took,
Rats half the manuscript have eat:
Dire hunger! which we still regret.
O! may they ne'er again digest
The horrors of so sad a feast.   *Prior.*

And India's woods return their just complaint,
Their brood decay'd, and want of elephant.   *Prior.*

How sleek's the skin! how speck'd the ermine!
Sure never creature was so charming!   *Gay.*

Like him I draw from gen'ral nature;
Is 't I or you then fix the satire?   *Gay.*

Had armed with spirit, wit, and satire;
And tipped her arrows with good nature.   *Gray.*

May yet ere noon-tide meet his death,
And lie dismember'd on the heath.   *Beattie.*

Where'er the oak's thick branches stretch . . .
Where'er the rude and moss-grown beech.   *Gray.*

Time, if we choose ill-chosen stone,
Soon brings a well-built palace down.   *Waller.*

Salt earth and bitter are not fit to sow,
Nor will be tam'd and mended by the plough.   *Dryden.*

NEKSHEB is our own!
'Tis done—the battlements come crashing down.   *Th. Moore.*

When round thy raven brow
Heav'ns lucent roses glow.   *Coleridge.*

Venus, all-bounteous queen! whose genial power
Diffuses beauty in unbounded store.   *Beattie.*

Love that 's forced is harsh and sour : . . .
To persist disgusts the more. *Barbauld.*

As thy waves against them dash . . .
Swallowed, now it helps to wash. *Cb. Lamb.*

Now cease my lute, this is the last
Labour that thou and I shall wast, *Wyatt.*

Lines not compos'd as heretofore in haste,
Polish'd like marble, shall like marble last, *Waller.*

Thus when the swain within a hollow rock,
Invades the bees with suffocating smoke. *Dryden.*

O hear our pray'r, O hither come,
From thy lamented Shakespeare's tomb,
On which thou lov'st to sit at eve,
Musing o'er thy darling's grave. *Warton.*

Better to hunt in fields for health unbought
Than fee the doctor for a nauseous draught. *Dryden.*

Just to thy fame he gives thy genuine thought,
So Tully published what Lucretius wrote. [wrought?] *Broome.*

Barren of every glorious theme, . . .
Producing subjects worthy fame. *Bp. Berkeley.*

                    and only now
In sorrow draw no dividend with you. *Crashaw.*

As if the place, the cause, the conscience gave
Bars to the words their forced course should have. *Daniel.*

As when his Tritons' trumps do them to battle call
Within his surging lists to combat with the whale. *Drayton.*

Alive, the hand of crooked age had marr'd
Those lovely features, which cold death hath spar'd. *Waller.*

And to love a martyr
Apollo followed arter. Warreniana.

BLANK VERSE.

Altho the next examples are given by their authors as blank
verse, they are just as good rhyme as some of the former.

Thou knowst that all my fortunes are at sea,
Neither haue I money, nor commodity *Sbak.*, M. of V.

E'en as the frogs, that of a wat'ry moat
Stand at the brink, with the jaws only out. *Cary's Dante*

Who builds on less than an immortal base,
Fond as he seems, condemns his joys to death. *Young*, Nt. 1.

To wonder; and too happy to complain!
Our doom decreed demands a mournful scene *Young*, Nt. 7.

Tho' quite forgotten half your Bible's praise!
Important truths, in spite of verse, may please: *Young*, Nt. 7.

They mortify, they starve, on wealth, fame, power,
And laugh to scorn the fools that aim at more. *Young*, Nt. 9.

The angel ended, and in Adam's ear
So charming left his voice, that he awhile
Thought him still speaking, still stood fix'd to hear,
Then, as new-waked, thus gratefully replied: *Milton*, P. L. 8, 1-4.

So sented the grim feature, and upturn'd
His nostril wide into the merkie air,
Sagacious of his quarry from so farr. *Milton*, P. L. 10.

I must begin with rudiments of art,
To teach you gamoth in a briefer sort, *Sbak.* Tam. Shrew, 3 : 1.

And from his horrid hair
Shakes pestilence and war. *Milton*.

His lot importunate in nuptial choice,
From whence captivity and loss of eyes. *Milton*.

His goddess Nature, wooed, embraced, enjoyed,
Fell from his arms abhorred; his passions died. *Pollok.*

        spread it then
And let it circulate in every vein. *Cowper.*

Ye vainly wise! ye blind presumptuous now,
Confounded in the dust, adore that pow-
'r And wisdom oft arraign'd. *Thomson.*

His near approach the sudden starting tear,
The glowing cheek, the mild dejected air, *Thomson.*

The evening star will twinkle presently—
The last small bird is silent, and the bee. *N. P. Willis.*

The air salubrious of her lofty hills
The cheering fragrance of her dewy vales. *Cowper.*

His wife, another, not his Eleanor,
At once his nurse and his interpreter. *Rogers.*

Not so the man of philosophic eye,
And inspect sage : the waving brightness he *Thomson.*

        goddess of the lyre,
Which rules the accents of the moving sphere. *Akenside.*

Of time and space and fate's unbroken chain,
And will's quick impulse; others by the hand *Akenside.*

Inapplicable as the last may seem, it is paralleled by Dryden's "allowable" rhyme in—

This office done she sunk upon the ground
But what she spoke, recovered from her swoon—*

---

* In Spenser's time this was proper—

    And cruddy blood enwallowed thay found
    The luckless Marinell lying in deadly swound. *F. Q.*

which is not equal to a similar one in Jeems Thackeray's
"Sonnick sejested by Prince Halbert gratiously killing the
stags at jack's cobug gothy."

> Some forty Ed of sleak and hantlered deer
> In Cobug (where such hanimals *abound*)
> Was shot, as by the newspaper I 'ear
> By Halbert, Usband of the British *crownd*.

The reader may also compare rhymes of *abroad* and *Lord*,
gone and *horn* (which the negro dialect requires) with the
blank verse ending *snores* and *nose* of another poet.

> Spurned not alone in walks abroad
> But in the temples of the Lord.　*J. G. Whittier.*

> And when the day is gone　. .
> Is hollowed out, and the moon dips her horn, *Longfellow.*

> 　　　　　a man who snores,
> Night-capped and wrapt in blankets to the nose.　*Alex. Smith.*

Prose.

The following examples were published as prose. The
first is from the English translation of Fouqué's Undine, p.
9, where the knight and fisherman

> enjoyed their chat as two
> such good men and true
> ever ought to do.

> The note of the cuckoo sounds in his ear
> like the voice of other years.　*Hazlitt.*

> The catbird* tunes his cheerful song
> 　before the break of day,
> hopping from bush to bush,†
> 　after his insect prey.　*Nuttall*, Ornithology, 1832.

---

　　　* often　　　　　　† with great agility

[And the trees]

If they sigh
for brigh-
ter skie-
s and for breez-
es with warm-   [Causes.
er breaths.   Prof. *Geo. Wilson* (M.D., F.R S.E.), Chemical final

It was so bright   It is well to dress
in his enemies' sight   in your best
that it gave light   when you go to press
like thirty torches.   a request.
          KING ARTHUR.   ATLANTIC MONTHLY, Dec. 1858.

Fondly do we hope,
fervently do we pray,
that this mighty scourge of war
may speedily pass away.   Prest. *Lincoln*, Mar. 4, 1865.

ALLITERATION.

Alliteration is related to rhyme, and is sometimes used to heighten the effect, but belletricians seem to be right in condemning it. The following selections are presented as examples.

Epochs . . . when sufferings and sorrows of startling severity are thickly sown in nearly every destiny, when terrible problems and terrible events leave little room for levity or leisure, are the very cradle and festival of the lyric muse —Edinb Rev., Jan. 1855, Art IV.

The rags and remnants of a robe which was a royal one once. *R. C. Trench*, on the Study of Words. (Superficial and inaccurate.) . . . . matter of more manifold instruction.—*Trench*, Select Glossary.

When beechen buds begin to swell   *Bryant.*

Lure on the broken brigands to their fate. *Byron.*

No gift beyond that bitter boon our birth. *Byron.*

. . . but the black blast blows hard. *Young*, Nt 8.

Cibber's brazen, brainless brothers stand. *Pope.*

But cull in canisters disastrous flowr's, *Garth.*

It is the common cant of criticism to consider, . . . *Hazlitt.*

Chimeras, crotchets, Christmas solecisms, *Tennyson.*

Wirst du doch noch nicht schämen. *Lessing*, Nathan der Weise.

Deep darting to the dark retreat. *Thomson.*

.   .   .   dive in dimples deep . . .
In deep dissimulations darkest night
Where gay delusion darkens in despair
Dawning a dimmer day on human sight
Undampt by doubt, undarken'd by despair. *Young.*

Inquiry into deeds at distance done. *Byron.*

And a dry dropsie through his flesh did flow,
Which by misdiet daily greater grew: *Spenser.*

. . . to dive into the depths of dungeons. *Burke.*

Down the deep dale and narrow winding way,
They foot it featly ranged in ringlets gay, *Beattie.*

And drives my dreams, defeated, from the field *Young.*

Wi' her freaks and her ferlies and phantoms of fear, *Hogg.*

From furrow'd fields to reap the foodful store. *Dryden.*

Flora floating o'er a bed of flowers. *Saxe.*

To fabling fancy forceful swell. *Charles Lloyd.*

unfortunate in the faults and follies of his forefathers, *Scott,*
Waverly 2, ch. 4.

A wandering, weary, worn, and wretched thing,   *Pollok.*

The faint fresh flame of the young year flushes   *Swinburne.*

And his glance follow'd fast each fluttering fair.   *Byron.*

Fantastic, fickle, fierce, and vain.   *W. Scott.*

We felt the full force of our folly.   *T. N. Talfourd.*

Warst uns bis hieher stecken Stab;
Sey's Vater fernerhin.   German Hymn.

And fever's fire was in his eye.   *W. Scott.*

And the green grasse that groweth they shall bren,   *Spenser.*

Full fathom five thy father lies.   *Shak.*

O hold that heavie hand,   *Spenser.*

A husky harvest from the grudging ground.   *Dryden.*

To hurt her hapless rival she proceeds,   *Garth.*

The hart hath hung hys old head on the pale   *Surrey.*

. . . . hear the happy hum of the busy bees.   *Langstroth,* Hive
                         and Honey Bee, 1853, p 355.

O'er stock and rock their race they take.   *W. Scott.*

But clothĕs meet to keep keene cold away,   *Spenser.*

Kypenihin kyynäswarsin,
Koprin kuumihin porohin   Kalewala, 6 :31-2, ed. Lönnrot, 1835.

Leaving his life-blood in that famous field.   *Rogers.*

With languid limbs in summer's sultry hours.   *Southey.*

Lo from Lemnos limping lamely,
Lags the lowly Lord of Fire   Rejected Addresses.

The lobuli of the liver are looser,   *Leidy* on Gasteropoda.

supreme mastery over the minds of men.   *W. C. Bryant.*

5

much more manifold meaning. *R. W. Emerson*, The Poet.

Amongst the teal and moor-bred mallard drives *Drayton*.

send him moping or maudlin to the mad-house. Rev. *Bellows*.

moon-blasted madness. *Coleridge*.

moaping melancholie and moon-struck madness. *Milton*.

ended their days in moping melancholy or moody madness.
Hazlitt, on Swift.

Taught mid thy massy maze their mystic lore. *Warton*.

But knights he now shall never more deface : *Spenser*.

Fresh with the nerve the new-born impulse strung. *Byron*.

LORENZO! hear, pause, ponder, and pronounce . . . .
We purchase prospects of *precarious* peace : . . .
O'er pleasure's pure perpetual, placid stream. *Young*.

Or where ill poets pennyless confer. *Garth*.

As pearls upon an Ethiop's arm. *Dyer*.

The clouds rise reddening round the dreadful height. *Barlow*.

The soul is on the rack; the rack of rest, *Young*.

The wise soothsayer, seeing so sad sight, *Spenser*.

A sable, silent, solemn forest stood. *Thomson*.

The cypress saddening by the sacred mosque. *Byron*.

To stern sterility can stint the mind. *Byron*.

Eve's wants the subtle serpent saw, *Gay*.

His steed stood still nor step would move. *Joanna Baillie*.

She makes silk purses, broiders stools, . . .
Paints screens, subscribes to Sunday-schools *Praed*.

The sirens will so soften with their song. *Chapman*.

And sink a socket for the shining share. *Dryden.*

Such sounds the Sibyl's sacred ear abuse. *Garth.*

. . . who can satiate sight In such a scene. *Young.*

My senses, soothed, shall sink in soft repose. *Young.*

> Thus when Philomela drooping
> Softly seeks her silent mate,
> See the bird of Juno stooping;
> Melody resigns to fate. *Swift,* 1773.

With short shrill shriek. *Collins.*

. . . and shov'd from shore. *Garth.*

Turns tenderly to some sweet simpering she. Arthur Brooke, 1818.

On tomes of other times and tongues to pore. *Byron.*

Bid thee to them thy fruitlesse labors wield. *Spenser.*

that though this ought to be. *Whewell,* Hist. Induct. Sci. 1, 75.

And Vernon's vigilance no slumber takes, *Garth.*

But that vain victory hath [!] ruin'd all. *Byron.*

For love, of whiche thy wo woxe alwaie more. *Chaucer.*

Of wine, or worse, in war and wantonness *Davors,* in Walton.

What woes await on lawless love. *Byron,* Corinth.

Never a white wing, wetted by the wave, *Byron.*

And, as he weaves his web of wiles. *G. P. Morris.*

That we were in a world of woe. *W. Wordsworth.*

Wikewästi wiilletellä,
Waskisissa waljahissa, Kalewala, 7 :437–8, ed. Lönnrott, 1835.

Waka wanha Wäinämönen, Kalewala, 10 :1. See also :290–1.

Da wirst du Herr von angesicht
   Zu angesichte sehen ;
Wie wohl wird dir bei diesem Licht
   In Ewigkeit geschehen.   *German Hymn.*

Stimulated to stupidity with excessive excitement.   *Montgomery.*

It was in freshest flower of youthful years, *Spenser.*

THE following stanzas, with the title FLIGHT OF THE FISHES, are published here with a view to protect them from unauthorised publication, an imperfect copy having got abroad.   The remainder may appear hereafter.

*   *   *   *   *   *   *   *

How envious of the rhymer would be Pope
and others who in rhyming could not cope ;
who could not entertain a transient hope
of leaving discords having equal scope
with *Rome* an' *dome* or *doom*, or *mop* and *mope*—
preferring cords as bad as *soup* and *soap*,
content with such as these to set a trope
since Bag of Rhymes they could not get or ope.

The poets link such sounds as *join, design*,
securing here and there a rhymeless line ;
and when from word to word they r rudely tost
delusion freely couples *boast* with *lost*,
remove with *grove*, or even *grove* with *love*
(as if nought else but lead were found above,)
care—car, with *war*, and also *wear* with *star*,
and like perversions truthful rhyme to mar.

*   *   *   *   *   *   *   *

MNEMOSYNE.

Weeds choke you, let Ameter* mow 'em   * The Reaper.
and Epilêsmonéstra† stow 'em   † The Oblivious.
with Epilêkythistra's‡ proem;   ‡ The Bombastic.
then give us *thoughts*, if you must grow 'em
to weave your tissues, or to sew 'em;
or try some bouts with rhymes, and show 'em,
to see if Dulot's muse will know 'em
as fit *bouts rimés* for a poem.

ERATO.

They say that "Some things can be done"   * Latin stȳlus,
(to quote Sam Patch) "as well as others"   as in stȳletto
and if you ca' nt take this advice   not στȫλος
I hope at least you l take my mother's;   as in peristyle.
for tho your lines may fish entice
they cannot tease my poet brothers,
whose polisht stile* reflects the sun
whilst your dull steel each glimmer smothers.

THALIA.

Aganophrosyne* is daft   * Kindliness.
in not excluding from your draft
that stuff about my friends your craft
would fret with Epileptôr's† shaft;   † The Censurer.
then let Gêthosyne‡ engraft   ‡ Delight.
ideas which the wȳnds might waft
oer Lethe on a smuggling raft
where charonades might rake 'm fore and aft.

REVIEWER.

Do you think your bag excuses?   Thou man of
Bag of Rhymes! which thus abuses   nought! what
in the stile of one who boozes   doeſt thou
evry poet who amuses   here, Unfitly
folk with fiction as he chooses?   furniſht with
buyer who his book peruses?   thy bag and
O that this head were Medusa's!   bookes! *Spenſer*,
or your robe were made like Creusa's.   bk. 3, c. 10, 24.

AUTHOR.

By such lays no poet loses
since no one himself accuses.

If I scoff, each muse confuses,
grants me no fish during cruises,
tempts with oafish lures and ruses,
tantalising him who uses
unrequited rhyme, that oozes
uninvited by the muses.

Author
offers a
valid a-
pology for
blaming
the poets.

EVPHROSYNE.

Vesperian litrature! an arid tract
where truth and virtue yield to narrow tact,
where men with children get the mind distract*
to leave them green-backt infamy.   In fact,
here Adikîa† has each law infract
but that of gain; and here, with lucre backt,
they buy up hacks with reputations crackt,
and try upon the public mind to act.

* he's much
diftract.
Shakefpeare,
Twelve
Night.
† Injustice.

MAGAZINIST.

Like chiffoniers we chuse to root in mire
for pelf, and jeer the muse for Plutus' fire;
and should THE WEAKLY CUTTER sneak a lyre,
the god* will meekly mutter—'Seek a liar—
'get brazen pens (and faces)—call me sire,
'let Phœbus' friends (the graces) all retire
'an' Chance supply the place with witches dire
'to dance around my mace in giddy gyre.'

* Mercury,
god of
thieves.

PUBLISHER.

My friends arouse ye! may yr aim be higher
than that of drowsy knaves ashamed of hire;
be not too proud for grubstreet fame to spire
when thus the crowd seeks this* well-named attire.
My Nerva's fowl—a thief—a lümergeir—
and not an owl, in brief, a tamer flier;
then get not *dearer* shams to please—or raise his ire,
but let yr *cheaper* flams appease a gracious buyer.

* Litter..
in yellow
covers.

MINERVA.

As when a jocky, caring not a jot
for aught but gold, and horses free to trot—
a showy (damaged) nag has cheaply got,
with skilful craft he hides the cheating spot,
and sells too well, a beast not worth a shot—
in which he imitates a specious lot
who with approv'd (but spurious) paper plot,
or literary frauds on paper blot;

who form a venal band, defraud the state,
and with the funds in hand, of morals prate—
or constitute a legislative tribe
who make the laws, yet itch to take a bribe;
the bony talons twitch at touch of gold
nor scarce forbear to clutch till all is told;
the coins as dropt excite the nervous grasp,
unclutcht that they may chink, in life's last gasp,

when Death's chill fingers crawl the neck around,
and throat and gold co-rattle in one sound.
> As when a minstrel girl is seen
> disporting with a tambourine,
> she moves her thumb in vibrant glide
> and gives a shudder to its hide,
> which makes its jarring discs of tin
> increase the stridulating din.

The carcas* stretcht, the frigid knuckles sink
upon the planks, and cause the gold to clink.
> As when an infant put to sleep
> is sinking in a slumber deep,
> the rattle which its wants demand
> · has ceast to sound within its hand,
> the jingling brass in rigid bone
> now falls, and yields its wonted tone.

* carkaffe.
Sbak.
carkas, carcas
Spenfer.
karkeis
Wiclif.

*   *   *   *   *   *   *   *

The cowboy now no more is found
to search intently where the ground
thrown up by worms in pellets round
thus simulates a tiny mound ;—
Now therefore is Lumbrîcŭs* wound
no more the fatal hook around
nor for an eelbob strung and bound ;
naught else he fears, and he is safe n sound.

*Loombreecoos, the fishing-worm.

There erst the lad for worms would dibble
   or list the brooks prosaic babble
when baiting hooks for fishes nibble
   or thoughtlessly in water dabble
unless arousd by Halcyon's treble,
   or noise of literary rabble
when wine-bought wit* begins to dribble
   oer throats relaxt for drink and gabble.

* . . . the trench-er fury of a rhyming para-site. *Milton.*

The schoolboy oft in days gone by
would cast a restless anxious eye
around the over-clouded sky
that signs of rain he there might spy.
How often would he deeply sigh
for rain enough to keep him shy
of school, that he might safely hie
a fishing, when he need not keep so dry.

Once he	fisht in	ev-er-y	streamlet
once in	ev-er-y	river	fisht he,
Ripping	up each	overtaskt	seamlet
which at	eventide	neatly	stitcht he,
Catching	of the	chub or the	breamlet
taking	fishes that	later	disht he,
Thus to	place his	name in a	reamlet
of some	littery	paper	wisht he.

FJNJS